Ladybug Girl

Ladybug Girl is a *New York Times* Best Seller

Who Can Play?

by David Soman and Jacky Davis
illustrated by Les Castellanos

Penguin Young Readers
An Imprint of Penguin Group (USA)

Who can play?

One can play.

One can play and play.

One can go up.

One can go down.

One can play and play all day.

But it is not so fun this way.

Who can play?

11

Two can play.

Two can play and play.

Two can go up.

Two can go down.

Two can play and play all day.

But it is not so fun this way.

Who can play?

Three can play.

Three can play and play.

Three can go up.

Three can go down.

Three can play and play
all day.

But it is not so fun this way.

Who can play?

Four can play.

Four can play and play.

Four can go up.

Four can go down.

Four can play and play
all day.

But it is not so fun this way.

Who can play?

We can play.

We can play and play all day.